*Every visible thing in
this world is put in the
charge of an angel*
— *St. Augustine*

For Skye, Merrick and Sedona – J. C.

For Megan, Ben, Emma, Julia and Rory – O. W.

Barefoot Books, Inc.
37 West 17th Street,
4th Floor East,
New York 10011

Text copyright © 2000 by Joanna Crosse
Illustrations copyright © 2000 by Olwyn Whelan
The moral right of Joanna Crosse to be identified as the author and Olwyn Whelan
to be identified as the illustrator of this work has been asserted

This book is printed on 100% acid-free paper

This book was typeset in Cochin 16pt
The illustrations were prepared in watercolor and mixed medium on 140lb watercolor paper

Graphic design by designsection, England
Color separation by Color Gallery, Malaysia
Printed and bound in Singapore by Tien Wah Press (Pte.) Ltd.

1 3 5 7 9 8 6 4 2

U.S. Cataloging-in-Publication Data (Library of Congress Standards)

Crosse, Joanna.
        A child's book of angels / written by Joanna Crosse ;
illustrated by Olwyn Whelan. — 1st ed.
[64]p. : col. ill. ;   cm.
Summary: The guardian angel of a curious little boy appears to him
one night to show him how every person, animal, plant and part of
nature is protected by an angel.
ISBN 1-84148-082-7
1. Angels -- Fiction. I. Whelan, Olwyn, ill. II. Title.
  [E] 21 2000   AC   CIP

A CHILD'S BOOK

of

ANGELS

written by

JOANNA CROSSE

illustrated by

OLWYN WHELAN

walk
the way of wonder...
Barefoot Books

Contents

Contents

Introduction

People have believed in angels since time began. The word angel comes from a Greek word, "angelos", which means "messenger", and angels are traditionally believed to bring messages to human beings to help them in times of difficulty. Some people also believe that there are protective angels taking care of all of the different life forms on the planet, and in the entire cosmos.

There are many famous stories of angels acting as messengers. Angels often appear as part of a dream, but in some cases angels make themselves visible to people while they are awake. One of the most famous examples of this was the appearance of the Archangel Gabriel to Mary, when he announced to her that she was to become the mother of Jesus.

However, angels don't always appear to humans in glorious robes with wings. An angel can also be a feeling, a color, a sound, or a smell. Even thoughts and words can be angels quietly giving you a message. Have you ever had an idea "out of the blue" and wondered afterward where it came from? Might it have been the voice of an angel? Whether you are aware of it or not, angels are with you all the time, and whenever you need to ask for help or advice, they will give you the message you need at that moment.

All over the world, artists, writers, musicians and ordinary people have tried to describe what it is like to meet an angel. As you travel through the pages of this book with Matt and his guardian angel Muriel, you will meet just a few of the many different kinds of angels that are a part of our cosmos. However young or old you are, I hope that this will help you to become more aware of the radiant presence of angels in your life.

Joanna Crosse

Beside each man who's born on Earth
A guardian angel takes his stand,
To guide him through life's mysteries.

— *Menander of Athens*

What Are Angels?

"What are angels?" asked Matt, as he climbed into bed.

"You see, there are all kinds of angels, Matt, more than you or I could ever imagine," said his mother. "And all of us have a guardian angel given to us at birth. That angel is by our side throughout our entire life."

"I've never seen my angel," Matt sighed. "So maybe I haven't got one."

"Most of us probably wouldn't recognize our guardian angel even if it did appear. Anyway, Matt, it doesn't really matter whether you can see yours or not – the most important thing is to remember that you've got one."

And with that, Matt's mother kissed him goodnight, turned out the light and shut the bedroom door.

Matt tossed and turned, wondering how he was going to get to sleep, and, if he did, hoping he wouldn't have another nightmare.

"Where are you, guardian angel?" he wondered. "What are you like? Do you have a name?"

Then, just as he was drifting into that space between waking and sleeping, he started to feel as though someone else was in the room.

Matt opened his eyes. There in front of him, sitting at the foot of his wooden bed, was the most beautiful being he had ever seen!

"Hello Matt, don't you know who I am?" asked the angel.

Matt was speechless.

"I've been appointed your guide for your time on Earth. Whether you knew it or not, I have been with you day and night ever since you were born."

Matt sat up, pinching himself quietly to make sure he was really awake.

"You know, it's quite funny that you have turned up like this because I was just wondering tonight how I could find out if I had a guardian angel."

"Well, that's why I'm here. Since you wanted to meet me, I decided to introduce myself. Angels don't usually appear unless they're invited to, or unless someone is in trouble or danger."

"Did you *choose* to be my guardian angel?"

"In a way, yes. I am much, much older than you, but you were born under the sign of Cancer, in June, and since that is also my sign, I was chosen to protect a child born under the same sign."

Matt thought about this for a while.

"Do you have a name?" he asked.

"I certainly do! My name is Muriel. Now, shall I start by telling you about the angels who rule the sun signs of the zodiac?"

"Yes, please!"

The Angels
of the Zodiac

"The word zodiac means 'the circle of life'.
Everything that happens on Earth, to plants
and to animals as well as to humans, is influenced
all the time by the movement of the constellations,
or groups of stars, and planets in the sky around us.
Many people measure time in years. One year is the
length of time it takes for the sun to travel through the
twelve major constellations, and these constellations
themselves each have particular qualities. They are
known as the signs of the zodiac and each one
is under the care of a different angel."

ARIES
21 March –
20 April
Machidiel

TAURUS
21 April –
21 May
Asmodel

GEMINI
22 May –
21 June
Ambriel

CANCER
22 June –
23 July
Muriel

LEO
24 July –
23 August
Verchiel

VIRGO
24 August –
23 September
Hamaliel

LIBRA
24 September –
23 October
Uriel

SCORPIO
24 October –
22 November
Barbiel

SAGITTARIUS
23 November –
21 December
Adnachiel

CAPRICORN
22 December –
20 January
Hamiel

AQUARIUS
21 January –
19 February
Gabriel

PISCES
20 February –
20 March
Barchiel

Angels and the Elements of Life

"Each sign of the zodiac is ruled by one of the four elements: earth, air, fire and water. These elements influence the characters of both the angels who rule each sign and the people in their care. Of course, the elements themselves are each under the care of specific angels, too."

The Fire Signs

"The fire signs are under the care of the Archangel Michael. These signs are Aries, Leo and Sagittarius."

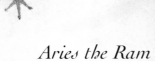 

Aries the Ram
21 March – 20 April
Aries is a passionate sign. Arians like to have adventures and are full of ideas; they are often courageous, dynamic and ambitious.

Leo the Lion
24 July – 23 August
Leos are big-hearted, enthusiastic and loving people. They are very creative and often have a wide range of interests. Leos can make excellent leaders.

Sagittarius the Archer
23 November – 21 December
People born under the sign of Sagittarius are cheerful and optimistic. They enjoy challenges and they cannot bear to be bored. They also enjoy exploring the meaning of life.

The Earth Signs

"The earth signs are under the care of the Archangel Raphael.
These signs are Taurus, Virgo and Capricorn."

Taurus the Bull
21 April – 21 May
People born under the sign
of Taurus are reliable, patient and
trustworthy. They have big hearts
and can be very charming. They like
stability and have a strong connection
to earth through their home
and work.

Virgo the Virgin
24 August – 23 September
Virgos are generally practical, tidy
and reliable and pay close attention to
detail. They are intelligent, analytical
types who strive for perfection in
everything they do.

Capricorn the Goat
22 December – 20 January
Ambition is a key trait of anyone
born under the sign of Capricorn.
Disciplined, patient and persistent,
Capricorns are also loyal, and have
a strong sense of humor.

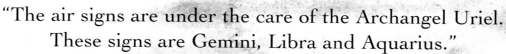

The Air Signs

"The air signs are under the care of the Archangel Uriel.
These signs are Gemini, Libra and Aquarius."

Gemini the Twins
22 May – 21 June
People born under the
sign of Gemini are excellent
communicators. They can be
witty companions, and their
natural versatility means
that they adapt easily to
most situations.

Libra the Scales
24 September – 23 October
Librans are usually sociable and
charming. They care deeply about issues
of justice and can be indecisive because
of their tendency to see both sides of
everything. Their main objective in life
is to create peace and harmony.

Aquarius the Water Bearer
21 January – 19 February
Aquarians often enjoy helping others.
They are positive about life and they
have a strong sense of independence.
They are fond of drama, which they
can play out in their everyday lives.

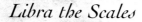

The Water Signs

"The water signs are under the care of the Archangel Gabriel.
These signs are Cancer, Scorpio and Pisces."

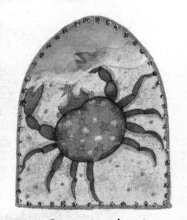

Cancer the Crab
22 June – 23 July
Cancerians are emotional and
intuitive. They are prone to mood
swings and can worry unnecessarily,
but they are very caring and make
excellent parents.

Scorpio the Scorpion
24 October – 22 November
Scorpio is a powerful, passionate
and determined sign. Scorpios can
be very competitive and are often
motivated by other people's success.
They enjoy life to the full and have
to be careful to use their energy
in an even way.

Pisces the Fish
20 February – 20 March
Pisceans are sensitive, kind and
caring. They are highly intuitive and
are often seen by others as being
dreamy. They can be so busy looking
after those around them that they
neglect to explore their
full potential.

The Planetary Angels

"It's like a kind of moving jigsaw, isn't it?" said Matt.

"You could say that, but you will find that there are more pieces than any of us, either angelic or mortal, could ever put together. The angels of the zodiac are very important, because they represent the different aspects of energy that give every living thing its unique identity, but there are many other angelic orders. Are you ready for an adventure?"

Matt nodded nervously. Within a fraction of a second, he was flying high in the sky at Muriel's side, as easily as if he had flown all his life.

"Now I'm going to introduce you to some

of the angels in your solar system. Let me
help you get your bearings.

"Look, you can see one of the
constellations I have just told you about.
That is Sagittarius!"

"But how were the planets and stars
formed?" asked Matt,

"Well, that's not an easy question. Nobody
really knows, so we had better start with
what we do know. The sun is the major
influence on the life forms on Earth, because
they are dependent on its heat and light. With
its waxing and waning, the moon influences
the growth of plants and the tidal movements
of the oceans on Earth. The planet you live
on is just one of the nine planets that orbit
the sun in your particular galaxy, but there
are many other planets and many other
galaxies in the universe – far more than
either you or I could begin to imagine."

The Angelic Hierarchy

"Now it's time for you to learn something about the orders of angels," announced Muriel.

"Sounds just like school to me," muttered Matt. "I thought angels were all the same, just with different jobs to do."

"Oh, no," said Muriel. "We have to have some organization up here as well as on Earth, otherwise there would be

celestial chaos. We'll start at the top!"

"All right," gulped Matt, who was beginning to feel a bit nervous. But at that moment he heard the strains of the most beautiful music, so wonderful he could feel tears well up in his eyes.

"What's that?" he gasped.

Muriel looked at him and smiled. "Come and meet the Seraphim and Cherubim," he said.

The Seraphim

"The Seraphim, whose name means 'fire maker', do much more than make music. As beautiful as it is, their music is just an expression in sound of the work they do in helping the Creator to pass down love and light through the other ranks of angels to all the creatures on earth. Their leader is Uriel."

Where the bright Seraphim in
  burning row
Their loud up-lifted angel trumpets
  blow,
And the Cherubic host in thousand
  choirs
Touch their immortal harps of
  golden wires,
With those just spirits that wear
  victorious palms
Hymns devout and holy psalms
Singing everlastingly.

— *John Milton*

The Cherubim

"The Cherubim, whose name means 'full of knowledge', are the voices of divine wisdom. Their task is to make sure that the universal laws are kept. The law of divine love requires you to love others for exactly who they are. The law of unity means that whatever you look like and wherever you come from, spiritually you human beings are all the same. And the law of karma means that any action you take, and even every thought that you have, has a result or a consequence, which will affect you as well as the person to whom it was directed. The leader of the Cherubim is Jophiel."

Look, how the floor of heaven
Is thick inlaid with patinas of bright
    gold:
There's not the smallest orb which
    thou behold'st
But in his motion like an angel sings
Still quiring to the young-eyed
    cherubim.
Such harmony is in immortal souls.

— *William Shakespeare*

23

The Thrones

"This group of angels is the Thrones. It's their job to see that divine justice is done in all situations and to keep cosmic harmony. They are peacemakers who help to bridge the gap between the visible and invisible worlds. Their leader is Japhkiel. Together, the Seraphim, Cherubim and Thrones make up the first tier of angels."

Around our pillows golden ladders rise,
And up and down the skies,
With winged sandals shod
The Angels come and go.

— *Richard Henry Stoddard*

25

The Dominions

"The Dominions are the first of the second tier of angels. This rank is in effect told what to do by the first band of angels that you've just met. The Dominions' task is to supervise the duties of the more junior angels. It is their responsibility to ensure that everything in the universe moves in accordance with the universal laws. The leader of the Dominions is Zadkiel. The Dominions work in the realm of spirit and don't get too involved in Earthly matters."

Silently, one by one, in
The infinite meadows of heaven
Blossomed the lovely stars,
The forget-me-nots of angels

— *Henry Wadsworth Longfellow*

The Virtues

"After the Dominions come the Virtues. These angels, who as you can see are particularly bright and radiant, are called 'the brilliant ones'. Their duties include organizing miracles and bestowing grace and courage on people who have forgotten who they really are. Sometimes, humans forget that they have access to all the help they need, if only they would remember to ask for it. The leader of the Virtues is Haniel."

For he will give his angels charge of you,
to guard you in all your ways.
On their hands they will bear you up,
lest you dash your foot against a stone.

— *Psalm 91: 11-12*

The Powers

"These angels are the Powers. They look after the divine plans and fight off evil spirits. When human beings need the strength to stand up for themselves or to resolve an unpleasant situation, without being hostile, they call for the aid of the Powers. The leader of these angels is Raphael. Together, the Dominions, the Virtues and the Powers make up the second tier of angels."

*B*e not forgetful to entertain strangers, for thereby some have entertained angels unawares.

— *Hebrews 13:2*

31

The Principalities

"The third tier of angels includes the Principalities, Archangels and Angels.
  The Principalities live up to their name in the sense that they are expected to set an example to the angels below them by living in accordance with the highest standards. Their task is to look after planet Earth and her countries and cities. Just like people, countries and cities all have guardian angels. When you are traveling to another place or if you get lost somewhere, you can call on the angel of that city or town to help you find your way."

I saw four angels standing
at the four corners of the earth
holding back the four winds.

— *Revelations 7:1*

The Archangels

"After the Principalities come the Archangels. Just as you can call on the angels of a place to help you when you are lost, so, too, you can call on the Archangels. There are different Archangels for different needs."

*M*ichael
is a protector and
guardian who helps
humans to oppose evil.

*G*abriel
is a messenger
and bringer of
good news.

*U*riel
is an angel of prophecy
who helps people to be
creative and to pass on their
knowledge to others.

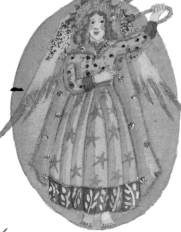

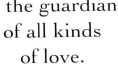

*H*aniel
is the guardian
of all kinds
of love.

*M*etatron
is the angel who helps bridge
the gap between the human
and divine realms.

*A*uriel
is the angel of the night
and the protector of
the Earth.

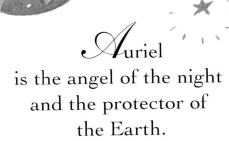

*R*aziel
is the guardian
of inner knowledge
and the mysteries.

The Angels

"If there are all these angels around us, why don't we see them on Earth?" Matt asked Muriel.

"Well, some people do see or feel their angels. But even if you don't sense angels around you, you need to know they're always there."

"What kind of angels look after the Earth?"

"Ah!" said Muriel. "That's exactly where I was going to take you next."

"Oh, I don't want to go back down there,"

said Matt. "I'm having such a lovely time
up here."

"Don't worry," replied Muriel. "Once you
have met the angels and the beings that work
more closely with humans and the planet, you
will find life on Earth much more fascinating
and magical than before."

And with that, they swooped down
through the night sky toward
planet Earth.

The Devas

"Imagine that everything in the world has a basic blueprint or pattern. It's up to all the angels to ensure that everything evolves as it should, in accordance with the cycles of nature, and they need some help to do that. So they work with Devas, whose name means 'shining ones', to help look after the mountains, rivers, seas, forests and fields. These Devas have many helpers, such as fairies, elves, brownies, sylphs and ondines. There are fairy folk everywhere on earth, working invisibly to support life. It is the responsibility of human beings to work with these Devas and angels. When people become greedy, though, they work against these forces. This is what creates most of the unhappiness that exists on your planet."

"Trees have always been known to contain great knowledge and power, because many of them have been around for a very long time and have absorbed so much wisdom from the Earth. So they are keenly watched over by the Devas. And like humans, trees have their own spirit guardians."

Angels, in the early morning,
May be seen the Dews among,
Stooping – plucking – smiling – flying –
Do the Buds to them belong?

Angels, when the sun is hottest
May be seen the sands among
Stooping – plucking – sighing – flying
Parched the flowers they bear along.

— *Emily Dickinson*

41

The Angels of the Seasons

In the wave of a wing, Matt found himself flying with Muriel straight toward a lush green hill. As they drew closer, an opening appeared and they both swept down a narrow tunnel into the most beautiful and fragrant garden Matt had ever visited. It was full of beautiful bright trees and plants with a little stream running through the middle. The birds seemed to sing more sweetly here than anywhere else, and the garden was full of butterflies and bees collecting nectar.

Muriel smiled as Matt gazed in wonder at the Devas of every plant and flower. "Most of the time you humans are probably

unaware of the invisible world of helpers in their gardens, fields and countryside. But there isn't a petal on a flower that isn't cared for by an angelic helper."

"Why do we have different seasons here on Earth?" asked Matt.

"Well, the seasons follow the cycles of birth, life and death – that cycle is the same for all of creation," Muriel explained.

"Are there guardian angels for spring, summer, fall and winter?"

"Yes, there are, Matt. Let's go and meet them."

Fall

"The guardian angel of fall is the
Archangel Michael. He looks
after the element of fire.

49

Michael helps the farmers with their harvesting.
He is the angel of courage and strength. He helps
people to reap rich rewards for their labors
earlier in the year and to celebrate
their achievements."

Winter

"The Archangel Gabriel is in charge of the winter months. As well as being a messenger of good news, he is often associated with winter celebrations.

He helps hold the Earth in balance between the fall and the spring. As the Archangel of truth and inner knowledge, he is the angel that nurtures future growth in the dark quiet of the soil. Gabriel is the Moon Lord and his name means 'Man of God'."

Spring

"The guardian angel of spring is the
Archangel Raphael, who is well known
for his healing powers.

$\mathcal{H}$is element is earth and his name means 'God has healed'. It is Raphael who helps the first shoots of flowers and plants to break through the earth, and he is also associated with the Tree of Life. He is the guardian and protector of all plants, great and small."

49

Summer

"The guardian angel of summer is the
Archangel Uriel. He is also the guardian
of arts and music and his element is air.
The name 'Uriel' means 'light'.

It is Uriel who oversees the laws of
karma and ensures that what we sow, we reap.
Uriel also helps humans to find their sunny side,
just as he helps the flowers, plants and trees
to blossom in the summer sun."

Angels of
Hearth and Home

When Matt found himself flying over
the chimney of his own house he felt a
terrible sense of disappointment. Had
his journey with Muriel come to an
end already?

Reading his thoughts, as angels so
effortlessly do, Muriel laughed.

"Don't worry, Matt, I've more to
show you yet. The reason we're visiting
your home just now is because I want
you to meet a rather special angel. In
fact, she's right behind you."

The boy turned around and gasped.
On the roof of his house, sitting just
above his bedroom window, was a
dazzling, white-robed angel who had
the sunniest smile he had ever seen.

"Greetings, Matt, I am the guardian angel of your home. Are you surprised? You shouldn't be. I've taken care of this house for nearly a hundred years – ever since it was built, in fact."

"What do you do all day…and night?" asked Matt.

"As you've been shown on your flight through the angelic realm, every single being in the universe has its own keeper or guide. So it's only right that your house should have an angel looking after it. Not only does the house need a watchful wing, I also help your guardian angels keep an eye on you and your two sisters, and your parents. None of us angels can work alone; we all rely on each other for help."

Angels of Birth and Death

"Do you have any questions you would like to ask me?" asked the angel, as Muriel sat beside Matt on the roof of the house.

"There is one thing I want to know, but I don't like to mention it," Matt said awkwardly.

"Why is that, Matt?"

"Well, my grandmother died last year and nobody at home wanted to talk about what had happened to her. I've been wondering where she went to."

"That's an excellent question, Matt. Lots of people on Earth look on death as an end, but it is really just a change. Whenever someone dies, an angel takes him or her across the bridge from the realm of Earth to the realm of spirit. In your Earth life, you are in a kind of overcoat that you've put over your soul. When it's time to go, you take the coat off and move on to the next cycle of existence."

"Can I see one of these Angels of Death?" Matt asked nervously, not entirely sure that he really wanted to meet one of them.

In front of him stood a glorious angel with the brightest colors around its being.

"You might think I don't particularly like my job, Matt, but helping humans to move across the bridge of death isn't as bad as it seems," said the angel. "Remember that many people leaving the planet are old, ill and weary of life – like your dear grandmother was. They are ready to move on and they are pleased to take off their raggedy

old coat and rediscover their radiant soul self. Of course, it can be very sad for people on Earth to lose their loved ones, particularly if their life has been tragically cut short. But death usually means the end of pain and suffering and the beginning of another adventure."

"So Granny could be at the beginning of another life by now?"

"That's right! All dying leads to new life, so it follows that all new babies have had some kind of existence before they are born. And just as I help souls who are ready to travel out of their Earthly existence, so the Angel of Birth helps souls who are preparing to travel in."

The Healing Angels

"Between the passages of birth and death, there are many occasions when people suffer illness. For those people, there are extra teams of healing angels. There are angels who work in hospitals with doctors and nurses, and in playgroups and school playgrounds when a child falls and hurts itself. All you have to do is to call on the angels to come and cheer you up. It's truly that simple. Just ask and one of us will be here. We can put our angel wings around you and make you feel much better."

Matt began to feel much better himself now that he was beginning to understand what a great help angels could be.

I have seen angels by the sick
   one's pillow;
Theirs was the soft tone and the
   soundless tread,
Where smitten hearts were
   drooping like the willow,
They stood between the living and
   the dead.

— *Anon*

"Matt, it's nearly time for me to leave you," said Muriel. "Take another look at the sky before you go back to your bedroom."

As Matt raised his eyes, he saw a sparkling, rainbow-colored network of light stretching above him from planet to planet and star to star. He understood for the first time that a truly fantastic network of celestial helpers interconnects all life. The night sky rang with the sound of glorious singing. Matt had never before felt so glad to be alive.

The next morning, Matt awoke to the sound of his mother drawing open his bedroom curtains.

"Did you sleep well? No more bad dreams, I hope."

"No, I asked my guardian angel to come and take care of me – and he did," said Matt with a broad smile on his face.

"You see, I told you all of us have a guardian angel. There's more to life than we see during the daytime."

Matt nodded, but not because of what his mother had said. He knew that from now on, with Muriel and a host of other angelic helpers by his side, his life would never be quite the same.

Sources

An Angel A Week, Ballantine Books, copyright Random House, New York, 1992

Angels – A Journal, Pomegranate Artbooks, San Francisco, 1995

Angels – A Joyous Celebration, Courage Books, an imprint of Running Press, Philadelphia and London, 1996

Barger, Jan, *In the Charge of an Angel – A Celebration of Angels in Pictures and Words*, Lion Giftlines, Oxford, 1997

Beilenson, Esther L., *Angels are Forever*, Peter Pauper Press, New York, 1994

Biriotti, Sophia (ed.), *The Possibility of Angels – A Literary Anthology*, Chronicle Books, San Francisco, 1997

Bloom, William, *Working with Angels, Fairies and Nature Spirits*, Piatkus, London, 1998

Davidson, Gustav, *A Dictionary of Angels*, The Free Press (a division of Macmillan, Inc.), New York, 1971

Gilded Angels, The, Charles Letts, London, 1993

Goddard, David, *The Sacred Magic of the Angels*, Samuel Weiser, Inc., York Beach, Maine, 1996

Goldman, Karen, *The Angel Book*, Simon and Schuster, New York, 1988/1992

Guiley, Rosemary Ellen, *Encyclopedia of Angels*, Facts on File Inc., New York, 1996

Hodson, Geoffrey, *The Brotherhood of Angels and Men*, Theosophical Publishing House, London, 1982

MacLean, Dorothy, *To Hear the Angels Sing*, Lindisfarne Press, Hudson, New York, 1990

Parker, Julia and Derek, *Parker's Astrology*, Dorling Kindersley, London, 1991

Sheldrake, Marianna, *The Crystal Healer*, The C.W. Daniel Company Ltd, Saffron Walden, 1999

Taylor, Terry Lynn, *Messengers of Light*, H.J. Kramer Inc., California, 1990

walk
the way of wonder...
Barefoot Books

The barefoot child symbolizes the human
being who is in harmony with the natural world
and moves freely across boundaries of many kinds.
Barefoot Books explores this image with a range of
high-quality picture books for children of all ages.
We work with artists, writers, and storytellers from
many cultures, focusing on themes that encourage
independence of spirit, promote understanding
and acceptance of different traditions, and
foster a lifelong love of learning.
www.barefoot-books.com